A FATHER LIKE THAT

by Charlotte Zolotow
Pictures by Ben Shecter

HARPER & ROW, PUBLISHERS

For Sidney Fields

I wish I had a father.
But my father went away
before I was born.
I say to my mother,
You know what he'd be like?
"What?" she says.

If he were here,
we'd leave the house together every day.

We'd walk to the corner
together.
And he'd go left to work.
And I'd go right to school.
So long, old man,
till tonight, he'd say.

When he'd come home at night, I'd meet him at the door.
He'd put his arm around me and say,
We made another day, the two of us,
and we'd both laugh.

He'd make a drink for you and a drink for him,
and he'd make you sit down
with him before dinner.

After dinner, we'd all do the dishes together
instead of just you and me,
and I'd do my homework.
When I got stuck, he'd show me how.

And pretty soon he'd say,
Hurry up so we can play
a game of checkers before bedtime.

But at bedtime
he'd say to you,
Oh, just one more.

When I'd be sick in bed,
he'd bring me home a new book
and tell you to lie down
while he sat with me and cheered me up.

He'd bring home good jokes from the office
and say, Hey, old fellow,
have you heard this?
And I'd tell it to all the kids the next day.

He'd rather go down to the store
and have a coke with me
than sit around having beer
with some other fathers.
He'd never call me sissy if I cried.
He'd just say, Never mind, old fellow,
you'll feel better later on.

He would come in the night
when I had nightmares
and talk to me.

He'd never show off about what a good father he was
at parent-teacher meetings.
And if Miss Barton told him I talk in class,
he'd say, Why sure, all boys do.

And no matter what happened,
he'd be on my side when things went wrong,
even if sometimes he had to say
it was really my fault.

When something bad happened,
I could always
talk to him.

His voice would be very low,
and when he was angry,
he would speak slowly and be kind.

He'd know all my friends by name
and ask something sensible like,

How's your dog?

He'd never joke about me to my friends
or say, Break it up, boys,
to send them home.

He'd understand why
I don't want to wear
that green shirt,
and he'd say to you,
You never were a boy.
You don't know.

He would wrestle with me, and when I wanted
he wouldn't mind if I pounced him a bit.
We'd listen to the doubleheaders together on TV.
When you'd say, Turn it down,
he'd smile and say,

If we make it lower, we won't hear.

And all the while
I'm telling this to my mother,
she is sewing very fast.
"I'll tell you what,"
she says, when I stop talking,
"I like the kind of father
you're talking about.
And in case he never comes,
just remember

when you grow up,
you can be
a father like that yourself!"